JED'S BAG

Jed has a big, red bag.

The bag has a tag on the zip.

Liz has a big bag.

It has a tag on the zip.

Liz and Jed run to
get the bus.

The bag is wet!
It is Liz's bag!

JUMPING JACK GAME

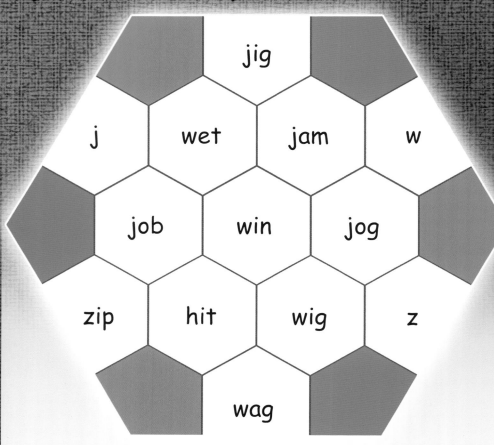

This is a game for two players. Each player has three counters, each set a different color. Players choose to be Red or Blue and place one counter on each of their colors. Players take turns to move a counter by sliding it into an adjacent space or by jumping over their opponent's counter into an empty space. When a player lands on a word, he/she must read the word aloud. The winner is the first player to get all three of his/her counters in a straight line.